HOW LITTLE
LORI
VISITED
TIMES
SQUARE

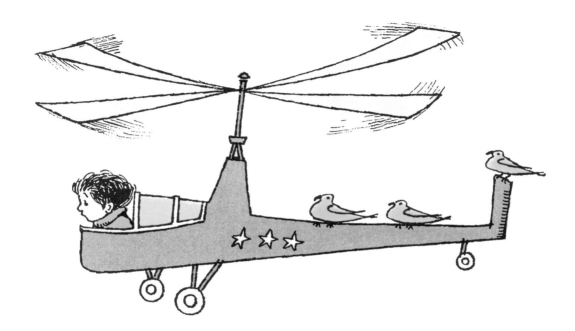

How Little Lori Visited Times Square

***

Written by Amos Vogel
Pictures by Maurice Sendak

***

*(This is a very funny book and should not be read
while drinking orange juice, or you will spill it!)*

***

HARPERCOLLINS PUBLISHERS · NEW YORK

To Steve

—— ✳ ——

One day Lori said to himself:
"I want to see Times Square."

So he walked to 8th Street
and took the subway
because
he wanted to see Times Square.

BUT WHEN HE GOT OFF, HE WAS AT SOUTH FERRY.

SO HE TOOK A BUS
BECAUSE
HE WANTED TO SEE TIMES SQUARE.

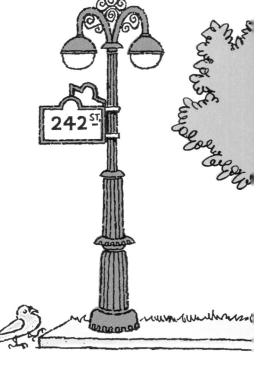

BUT WHEN HE GOT OFF THE BUS,
HE WAS ON 242ND STREET.

So he took a taxi
because
he wanted to see Times Square.

The driver said: "Do you have enough money to pay me?"

Lori said: "What a silly question! I am much too little to have enough money for a taxi."

So the driver said: "Please get out then."

So Lori took the elevated subway because
he wanted to see Times Square.

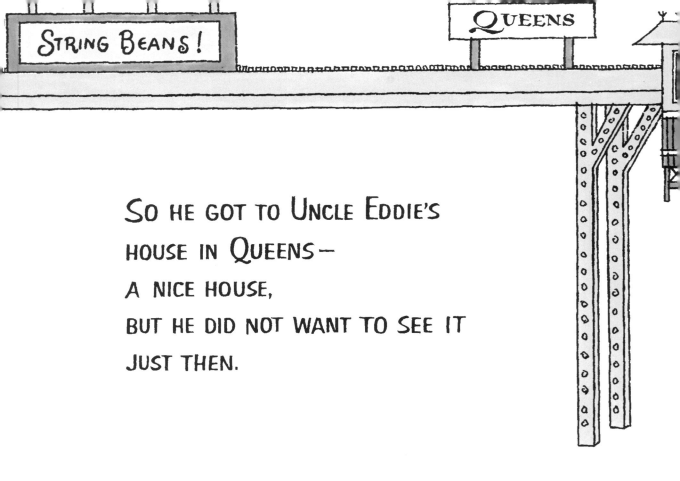

STRING BEANS!

QUEENS

SO HE GOT TO UNCLE EDDIE'S
HOUSE IN QUEENS —
A NICE HOUSE,
BUT HE DID NOT WANT TO SEE IT
JUST THEN.

(A LOT OF THINGS HAPPEN NOW, SO WE HAD BETTER START UP HERE....)

SO HE TOOK A BOAT TO SEE TIMES SQUARE
AND GOT TO STATEN ISLAND.

So HE TOOK A HELICOPTER TO SEE TIMES SQUARE AND
GOT TO IDLEWILD AIRPORT.

So HE TOOK A RIDE ON A HORSE AND WAGON AND
GOT INTO THE MIDDLE OF CENTRAL PARK.

SO HE JUMPED ON A PONY BUT ONLY RODE AROUND IN A CIRCLE.

So HE JUMPED IN WITH THE SEA LIONS AND
ASKED THEM TO TAKE HIM TO TIMES SQUARE,
BUT ALL HE GOT — WAS WET.

So HE FINALLY TOOK AN ELEVATOR TO GET TO
TIMES SQUARE, BUT ALL HE GOT TO WAS
THE 125TH FLOOR OF MACY'S. ————————>

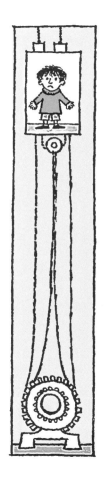

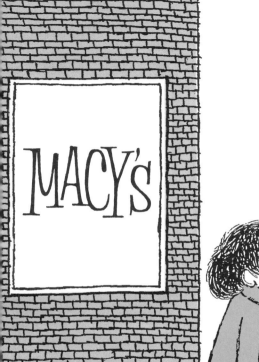

So HE SAT DOWN ON THE SIDEWALK AND CRIED.

SUDDENLY A TURTLE WALKED BY AND SAID:

WHY

ARE

YOU

CRYING

MY

LITTLE

FRIEND

So Lori cried some more and said:
"Because I want to see Times Square,
I took a subway and got to South Ferry,
and a bus and got to 242ND Street,
and a taxi, and the man told me to get out,
and the elevated subway and I got to Queens,
and a helicopter to Idlewild,
a horse and wagon to Central Park,
and an elevator to Macy's, where I am now,
although I do not want to be here."

AND THE TURTLE SMILED
(IF YOU CAN IMAGINE A TURTLE SMILING!)
AND SHE SAID:

DO NOT

WORRY MY LITTLE

FRIEND JUST HOP

ON AND I

WILL TAKE YOU

TO

TIMES SQUARE

So Lori got on, and the turtle started crawling (very slowly of course).

AND THIS WAS

FOUR MONTHS AGO—

AND NOBODY HAS HEARD FROM THEM SINCE......